When the Bees Fly Home

Andrea Cheng · Illustrations by Joline McFadden

TILBURY HOUSE PUBLISHERS · THOMASTON, MAINE

The beeswax is smooth. I pass it from hand to hand until it is soft enough to mold. Then I form the shimmering wings of a honeybee.

In flight, a bee's two pairs of wings move 180 times per second, but it only flies at about 15 miles per hour. A dragonfly can fly twice as fast. A honeybee has five eyes!

Dad calls me. "Jonathan, come and unload these supers." So I set my bee down gently in a corner of the truck and jump to the ground.

Dad is silent as he works. The muscles in his arms bulge and shine with sweat. His face strains with the weight of the supers and the stress of this dry spell.

Suddenly I drop a super on my toe and cringe as I wait for the pain to hit.

"Get back in the truck," Dad orders. I go but still I hear him mutter.

He says I might as well stay home. I am no help at all.

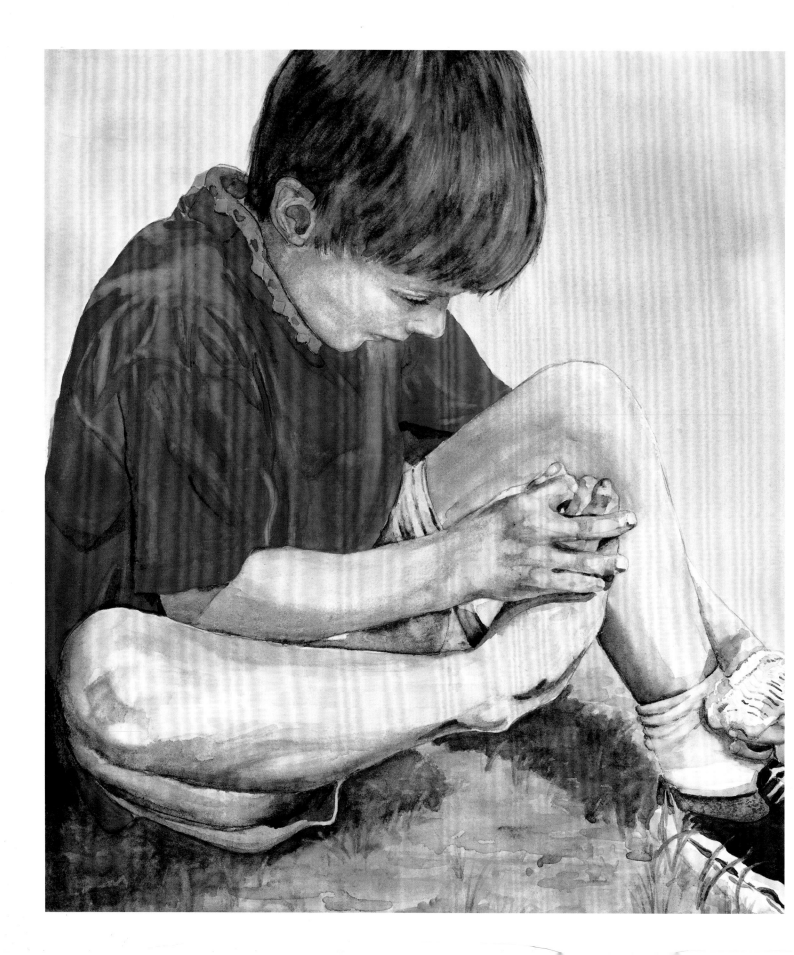

As I inspect my swollen toe, I know Dad is right. My arms are so skinny—even my four-year-old brother is stronger. He likes to say that he is a beekeeper like Dad. He goes around the house wearing a sheet like a bee veil and pretending to smoke the hives. Not me. I just want the wax.

Dad heads off toward the hives without even a word to me. I think at first of following him to see the honeybees come and go as they fly around the hive. I like to watch them, and sometimes I see them do their dance. But my toe is throbbing. I stay in the truck and form the thick body and tiny legs of my wax bee.

Worker bees do a special "waggle" dance to give the other workers directions to where there are flowers with lots of pollen or nectar. They dance faster if there is so much nectar that they need more bees to bring it in. The dance tells the other worker bees the direction and distance to the flowers.

When Dad comes back he is mad because he got stung under his eye. But I think he feels bad about my toe because he tosses me a big glob of fresh wax for the ride home and offers me a drink of ice tea from the thermos.

Dad says that the dry spell has gone on so long that the honey will be slim this year. The clover blossoms are small and few. The locust flowers are wilting in the sun. That means less money than the little we already have. We pass the ice cream store and I hope for a second that Dad will stop because of my toe but instead he speeds up.

Each hive has one queen bee who lays about 1,500 eggs per day (in the summer), thousands of female worker bees who do all the work and guard the hive, and several hundred male bees, called drones, who live in the hive until they are needed to mate with a new queen from another hive.

When we pull in Mom is working in the garden. My brother Nicholas runs to the truck and I see Dad smile like he never does at me as he picks up his sturdy son. Mom knits her brow when she sees me hop.

"What happened?" she asks.

"Dropped a super on my toe," I say, sitting down in the grass.

During the honey-gathering season there are 40,000 to 60,000 bees in a beehive. Worker bees live for about 35 days. It has always been thought that bees do not sleep, but new research suggests that they do. Our knowledge of these amazing insects continues to evolve.

Mom gets ice wrapped in two checkered towels to hold on my toe, then she waits to see what I have made today. She picks up the bee carefully and turns it around in her hand.

"Perfect," she says. I know she will put it on the shelf by her bed with the other tiny wax animals—a cow with its calf, a pair of geese. I know she looks forward to each new addition.

For a hive to make two pounds of honey on a good day, its worker bees will fly 110,000 miles and bring back nectar from 4 million flowers. Each bee can carry half her body weight in pollen and nectar.

As bees gather nectar and pollen, they brush the pollen against the female part of a plant so that it produces seeds—or fruit or vegetables. Much of the food that we eat grew because it was pollinated by bees.

Mom looks over at Dad. "How was the day?"

Dad doesn't answer, so I do. "The same," I say.

She points to the drooping parsley. "I watered this morning and look."

I nod.

Only Nicholas doesn't seem to care about the dry spell. He shows Dad how strong he is getting. Dad feels his muscle and says yes, it really is very big.

That night my toe throbs and I cannot sleep. I think about the bees. They are getting sluggish. Their dances are slow. Only Dad works in a frenzy. I get up and hop into the kitchen to get more ice.

The first common honeybees in North America were brought by the Pilgrims to pollinate their apple trees. Native Americans called these honeybees the "white man's fly."

There is Mom at the stove.

"What are you doing?" I ask.

"Making candles," she says. The smell is sweet like the wax I always mold in my hands. "Tomorrow is the farmer's market. I will try to sell a few." She pours the wax into small square molds. When it hardens, I take them out and set them in a line on the table. Ordinary candles. I make a tiny chick with a drip of wax. Suddenly I have an idea.

Bees bring nectar back to the hive in their special "honey stomachs" and give it to house bees in the hive, who store it in empty cells. Enzymes from the bees and evaporation concentrate the nectar into honey.

"How about I decorate your candles?" I say. I make a family of tiny wax ducks and press it onto the top of a candle. Then I form a few small honeybees and arrange them around the side of a candle. I make the candle into their home.

"The bees are flying into the hive to avoid the rain," I tell Mom.

Mom strokes my skinny arm. She adjusts the ice on my toe. "Better?"

I nod.

Worker bees build honeycomb with wax they secrete from their abdomens. They build hexagonal cells to store honey or pollen and to raise baby bees, and peanut-shaped cells to raise queen bees.

By morning the table is covered with our animal candles. Dad gets up before the sun and looks over our work. He picks up the candle with the bees.

"Do you think we could save this one?" he asks.

"What for?" I ask.

"For me," he says, putting it on the windowsill. Then he looks more closely at how I have arranged the bees near the entrance of the hive. Together we look out the kitchen window. The sun is rising between thick gray clouds. The air is heavy.

"Your bees may know something we don't," he says.

Bees cluster around the queen in the hive during a cold winter, eating honey, vibrating and trading places to keep warm. They maintain a temperature of 90 degrees even on the coldest of winter days. To cool the hive in hot weather they bring water into the hive and evaporate it by fanning their wings.

Our candles sell fast. By ten o'clock there are no more. Our coffee can is full of money. A lady stops at our empty table. "Got any more?" she asks.

I shake my head.

"All sold out," says Mom.

"Can I place an order then? What I'd like is a snail candle."

I write that down and tell her I'll have it next week. By noon we have more than forty new orders.

When Dad comes home, we show him our heavy coffee can and my order sheet. He can hardly believe it. He stays up late with me and Mom as we work on our next batch of candles.

"Amazing," he says as I form the antennae of a snail and then stick it on the candle. Dad lights the wick of his bee candle.

"The bees were flying home all day today, Jonathan," he says.

Wild bees will make their home in a hollow tree or between the walls of a building. The modern hive box, called the *Langstroth hive,* was patented in 1852 and is designed so that the honey can be removed without killing the bees or destroying their home.

This time we make even more candles—with turtles and frogs and doves. Dad holds the extra wax in his hands so it will be warm and easier to mold. Suddenly we hear a sound like tapping on the window. I look at Dad. He picks up the bee candle and the three of us go out to the front porch. The raindrops are big and far apart at first, but in a few minutes it is pouring.

"I'm going in," Mom says. "Just like the bees, I go in when it rains."

Bees communicate by *pheromones,* or smells. Each bee colony has its own distinctive odor, and its bees can recognize hive members or robber bees by smell. When a beekeeper "smokes" the hive, it masks the smell so the bees can't communicate the "alarm" pheromone. When a worker bee stings, she dies afterward because her stinger is barbed, and she can't pull it out without tearing her abdomen. Male bees, or *drones,* do not have stingers.

We hear the screen door slam. Then a gust of wind blows out the candle, but Dad and I are not ready to go in yet. We walk into the darkness of our front yard.

"Your bees were right," Dad says. Then we just stand there with our arms touching, feeling the water run down.

The survival of a bee colony depends upon thousands and thousands of bees working together, each one doing its job.

ABOUT HONEYBEES

(The editors thank the Maine State Beekeepers Association for their highly informative website, from which some of this book's facts about bees were drawn. Thanks also to beekeeper and environmental consultant Tim Forrester for his technical review.)

Of the many species of bees, only nine make honey, and they are amazing insects. Honeybees have been around for 100 million years, and the practices of beekeeping and honey collection date back 4,000 years, yet honeybees were unknown in North America until carried here by settlers from Europe.

Ancient Egyptians paid taxes with honey, and Alexander the Great's body was embalmed with it. Honey speeds the healing of open wounds, contains vitamins and antioxidants, and is fat free, cholesterol free, and sodium free. Honey stored in the tomb of King Tut—to nourish him in the afterlife—was still edible after 3,000 years, because it never spoils. It is the only food that contains all the substances necessary to sustain life (including water).

Honeybees account for 80% of all insect pollination, making them critical for the production of many fruits and vegetables. One-third of a typical human diet consists of foods that rely on honeybee pollination for their production!

That is why the phenomenon known as *colony collapse disorder* (CCD) is so disturbing. In CCD, the hive's worker bees disappear, leaving behind food, the queen, and a few nurse bees to care for the queen's offspring. CCD has increased in recent years, both in North America and in Europe, for reasons that are still poorly understood. Causes may include pesticides, habitat loss, and beekeeper practices, but the single greatest threat to honeybees is a parasitic mite from Asia called *Varroa destructor.*

A Varroa mite is smaller than a pinhead and crawls onto an immature bee while it is developing within its brood cell in the hive. The mite chews a hole in the bee's exoskeleton in order to suck its blood, and the wound does not heal. That weakens the bee's immune system and eventually causes the entire colony to be vulnerable to stress and disease. Beekeepers are forced to treat hives with chemicals in order to control the Varroa population in the hive.

Healthy populations of honeybees are critical to agriculture, biodiversity, and the health of our planet. Long live honeybees!

TILBURY HOUSE PUBLISHERS

12 Starr Street, Thomaston, Maine 02861

800–582-1899 • www.tilburyhouse.com

First paperback printing: October 2015 • 10 9 8 7 6 5 4 3 2 1

To my brother, the bee man. —A. C.

Library of Congress Cataloging-in-Publication Data

Cheng, Andrea.

When the bees fly home / Andrea Cheng ; illustrated by Joline McFadden.

p. cm.

Summary: The son of a beekeeper, Jonathan is not sturdy enough to do some of the work, but with the support of his mother he finds a way to help the family and form a bond with his father. Includes bee facts.

ISBN 0-88448-238-3 (Hardcover : alk. paper)

[1. Beekeepers—Fiction. 2. Bee culture—fiction. 3. Honeybees—Fiction.] I. McFadden, Joline, ill. II. Title.

PZ7.C41943 Wh 2002

[E]—dc21   2002001253

Design by Geraldine Millham, Westport, Massachusetts

Editorial and production: Jennifer Elliott, Audrey Maynard, Barbara Diamond

Color separations and film by Integrated Composition Systems, Spokane, Washington

Printed by Shenzhen Caimei Printing Co., Ltd. in Shenzhen, China

54924-0 (August 2015)

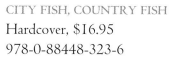

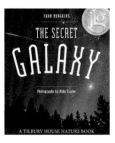

THE SECRET GALAXY
Hardcover, $16.95
978-0-88448-391-5
- Junior Library Guild selection
- "Highly recommended."
  –Seymour Simon, recipient
  of the AAAS/Subaru Lifetime
  Achievement Award
- "Opens doors for a variety
  of uses in the school setting…"
  –National Science Teachers
  Association

SWIMMING HOME
Hardcover, $16.95
978-0-88448-354-0
- "Susan Shetterly writes with an
  elegance of expression that takes
  my breath away."
  –Monica Wood, author,
  When We Were the Kennedys
- "Raye's soft, bright paintings
  depict the journey, varying
  perspective to give readers
  a sense of drama."
  –*Kirkus Reviews*

THE PIER AT THE END OF THE WORLD
Hardcover, $17.95
978-0-88448-382-3
- Skipping Stones Honor Award
- "A visual and verbal delight for
  adults and children."
  –National Science Teachers
  Association
- "Presents an amazing amount
  of marine biology in an
  engaging and educational way."
  –Jerry R. Schubel, President,
  Aquarium of the Pacific, Long
  Beach, CA

A CARIBOU ALPHABET
Paperback, $8.95
978-0-88448-446-2
- ALA Notable Book
- Ten Best Illustrated Books,
  Parenting magazine
- "A tour de force: both a
  homage to a particular animal
  and a textbook example of how
  an alphabet book can educate
  and delight a young reader."
  –*New York Times*

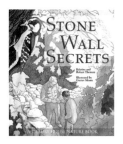

STONE WALL SECRETS
Paperback, $8.95
ISBN 978-0-88448-229-1

THE VERY BEST BED
Paperback, $8.95
978-0-88448-410-3
- "Raye's light-infused watercolors
  richly complement this gentle
  story." –*School Library Journal*

ANDREA CHENG teaches English as a Second Language and writes children's books in Cincinnati, Ohio, where she lives with her husband and their three children. She is the author of *The Year of the Book, Grandfather Counts, Only One Year,* and other books for young readers. The idea for *When the Bees Fly Home* came from observing her brother, who is a beekeeper and bee inspector in Southern Ohio.

JOLINE MCFADDEN is a retired high school biology teacher who lives in Lewiston, Maine. An accomplished watercolorist, this is her first children's book.

TILBURY HOUSE PUBLISHERS
12 Starr Street, Thomaston, Maine 04861
800–582–1899 • www.tilburyhouse.com